OPHELIA HOUSE

ORIGINAL ARTWORK

ANDREW L. WILLIS

CREATED AND WRITTEN

CARLTON L. SAMPSON
COVER DESIGN, BALLOONS, PAGE LAYOUT

Palanquin

STATION MANSION GARDENS
CARRIAGE HOUSE

*PO LYN LEE "OPHELIA HOUSE" EPISODE 3 "LADY LIBERTY" PAGE 23.

THE COLONIAL HOTEL
1776 BENJAMIN FRANKLIN PARKWAY PHILADELPHIA, PENNSYLVANIA
FRIDAY 8:38 PM EASTERN STANDARD TIME

♫AND INTERVIEWS WITH RENE LABEWLA HONOLULU POLICE ARE SAYING RENE LABEWLA'S ABDUCTOR AND THE SNIPER, WERE THE SAME MAN.♫*

TEN TO TWELVE YEARS OLD, NO OLDER.

RIGHT, TWELVE THIRTY. HER NAME WILL BE SUZIE.

I AM HERE TO TAKE YOUR TRAY...AND THIS PACKAGE, CAME FOR YOU, SIR.

SURE, JUST PUT THE WINE ON THE TABLE.

VERY GOOD, SIR.

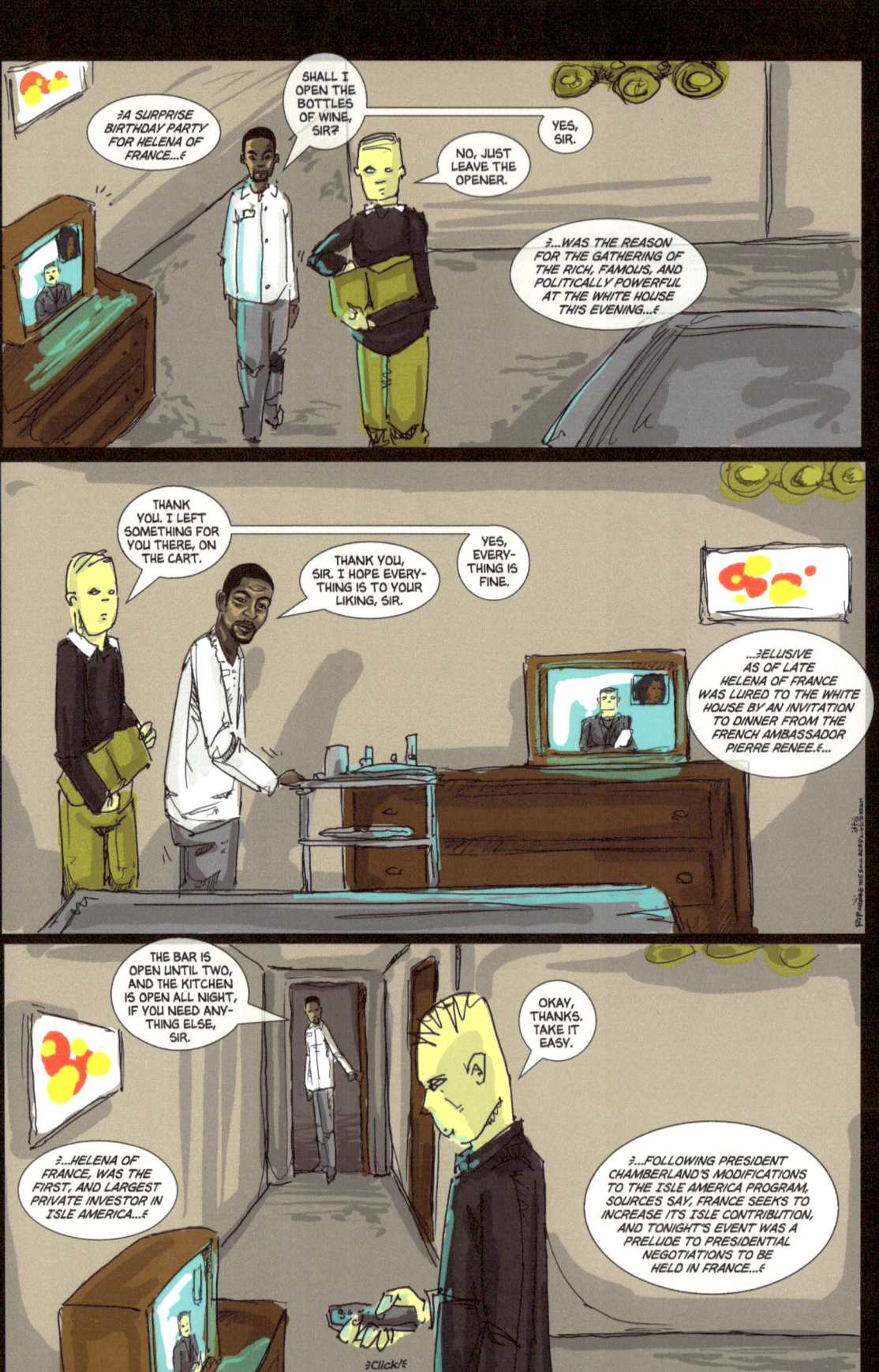

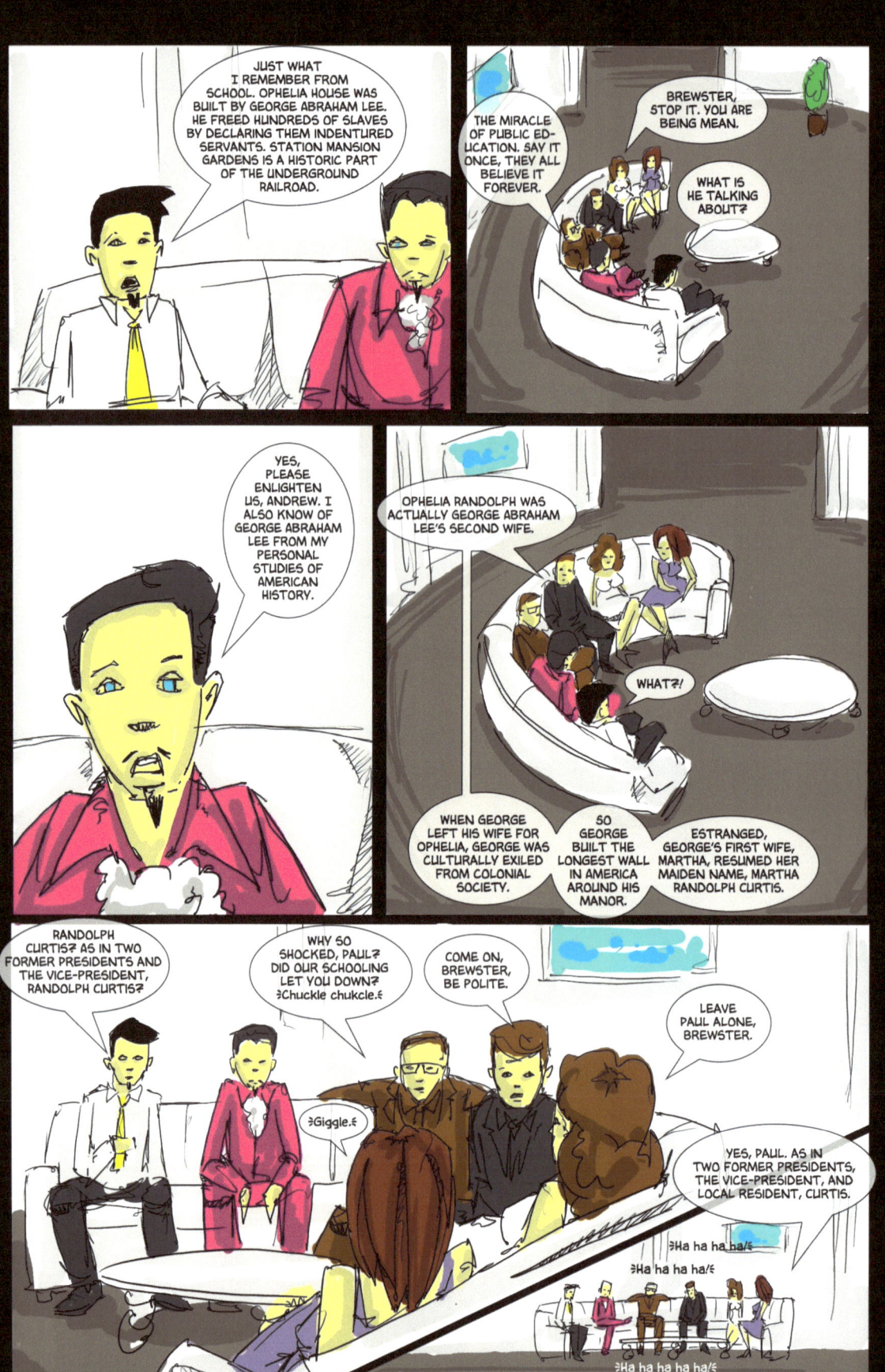

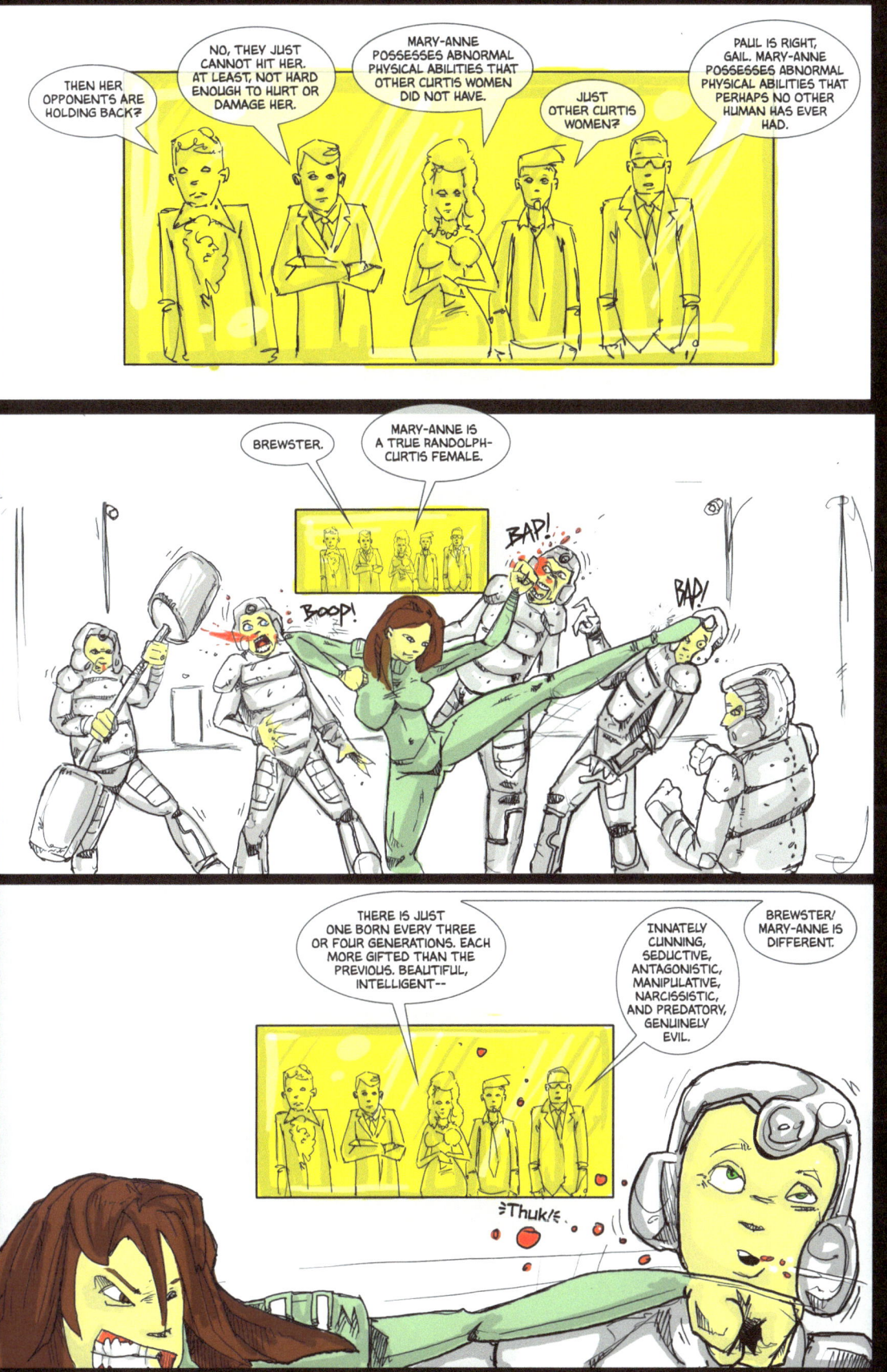

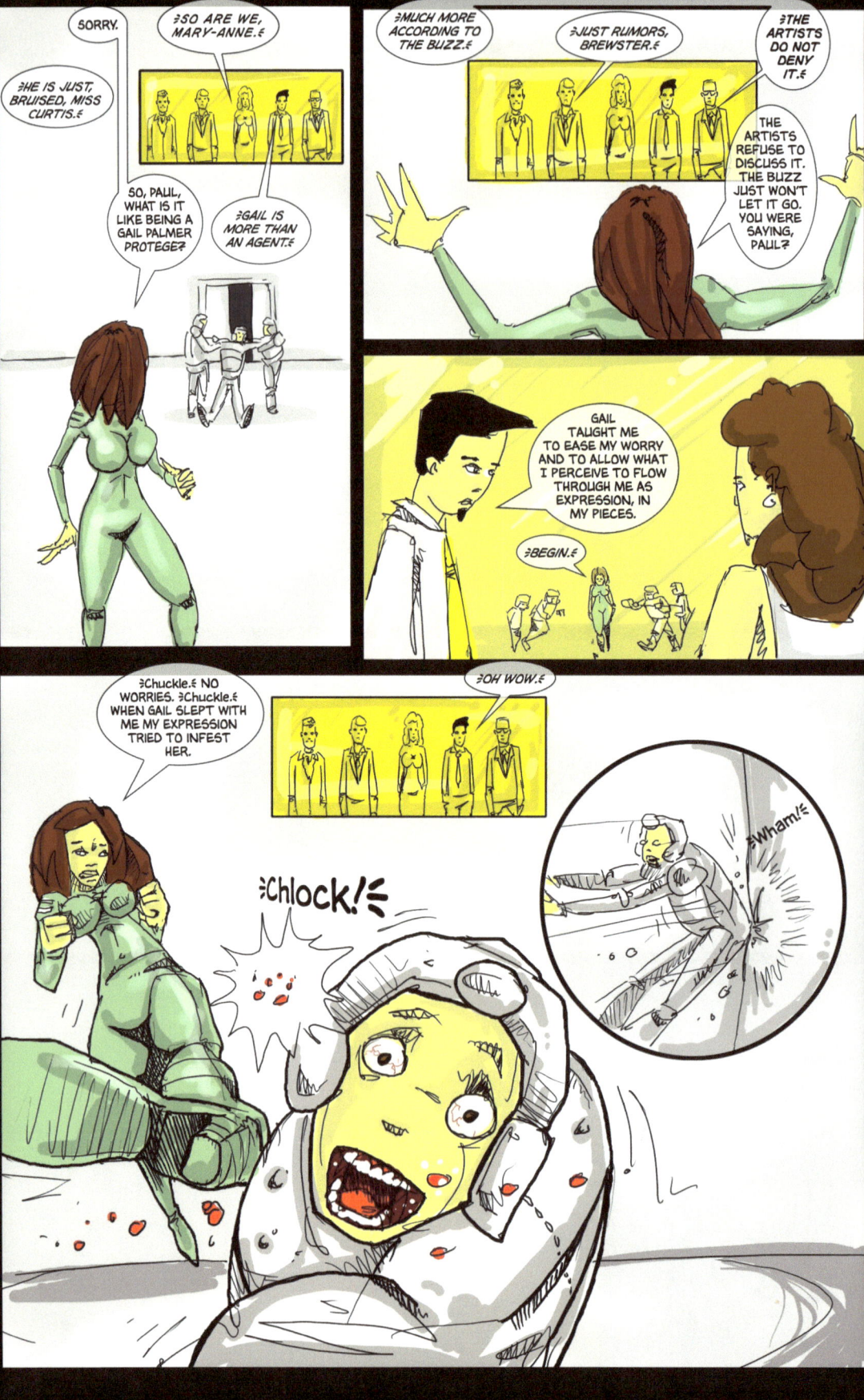

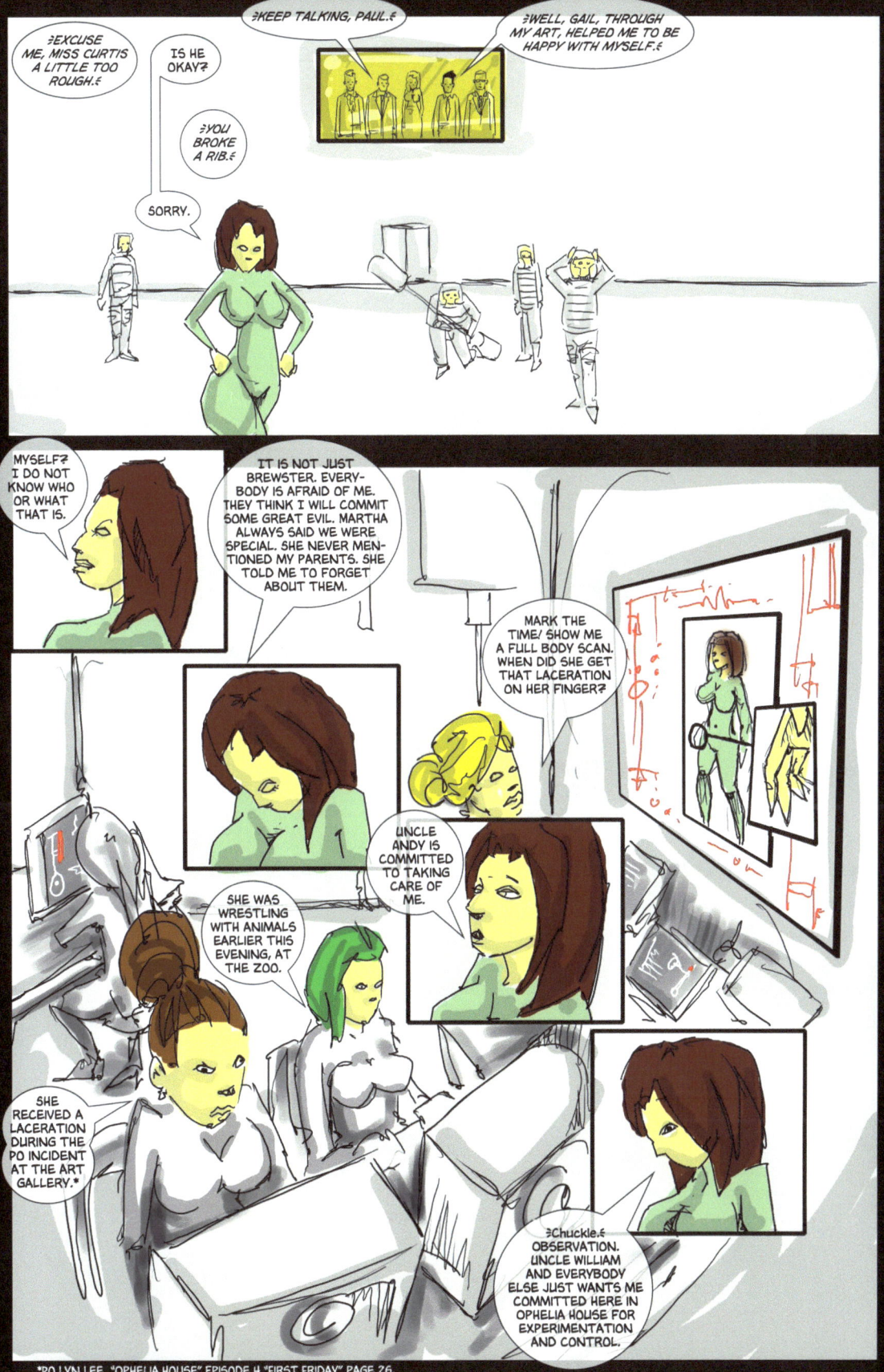

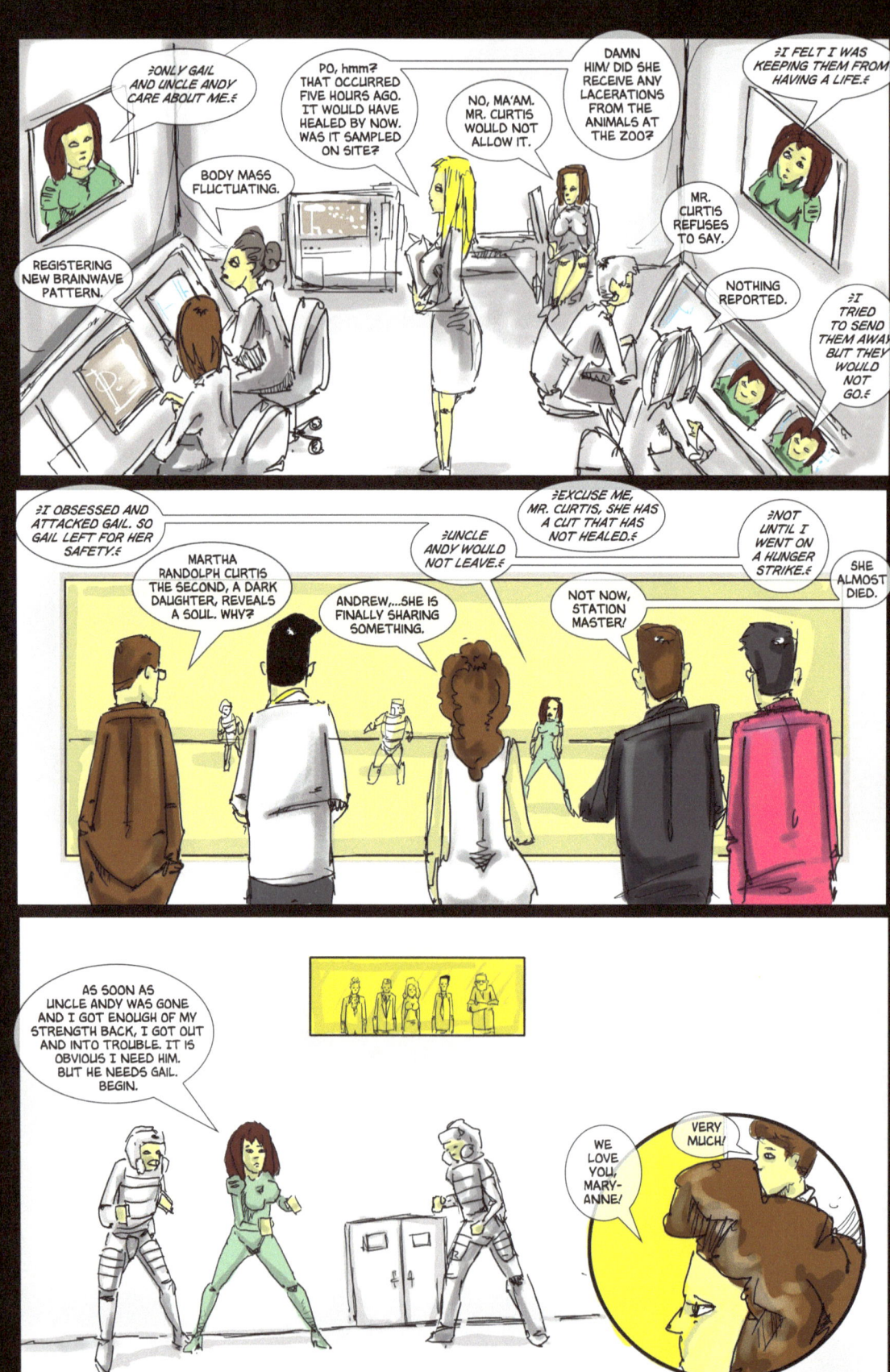

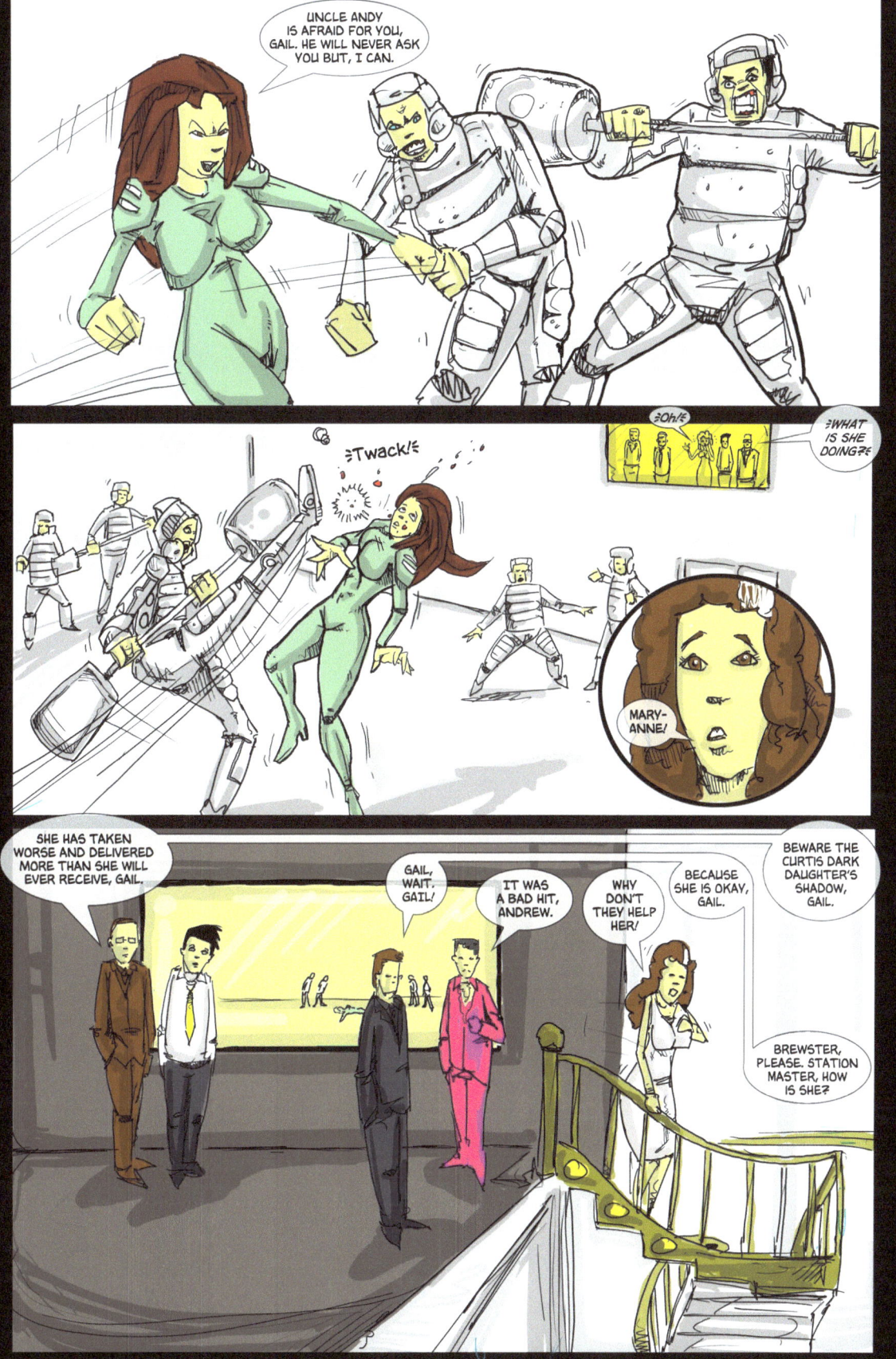

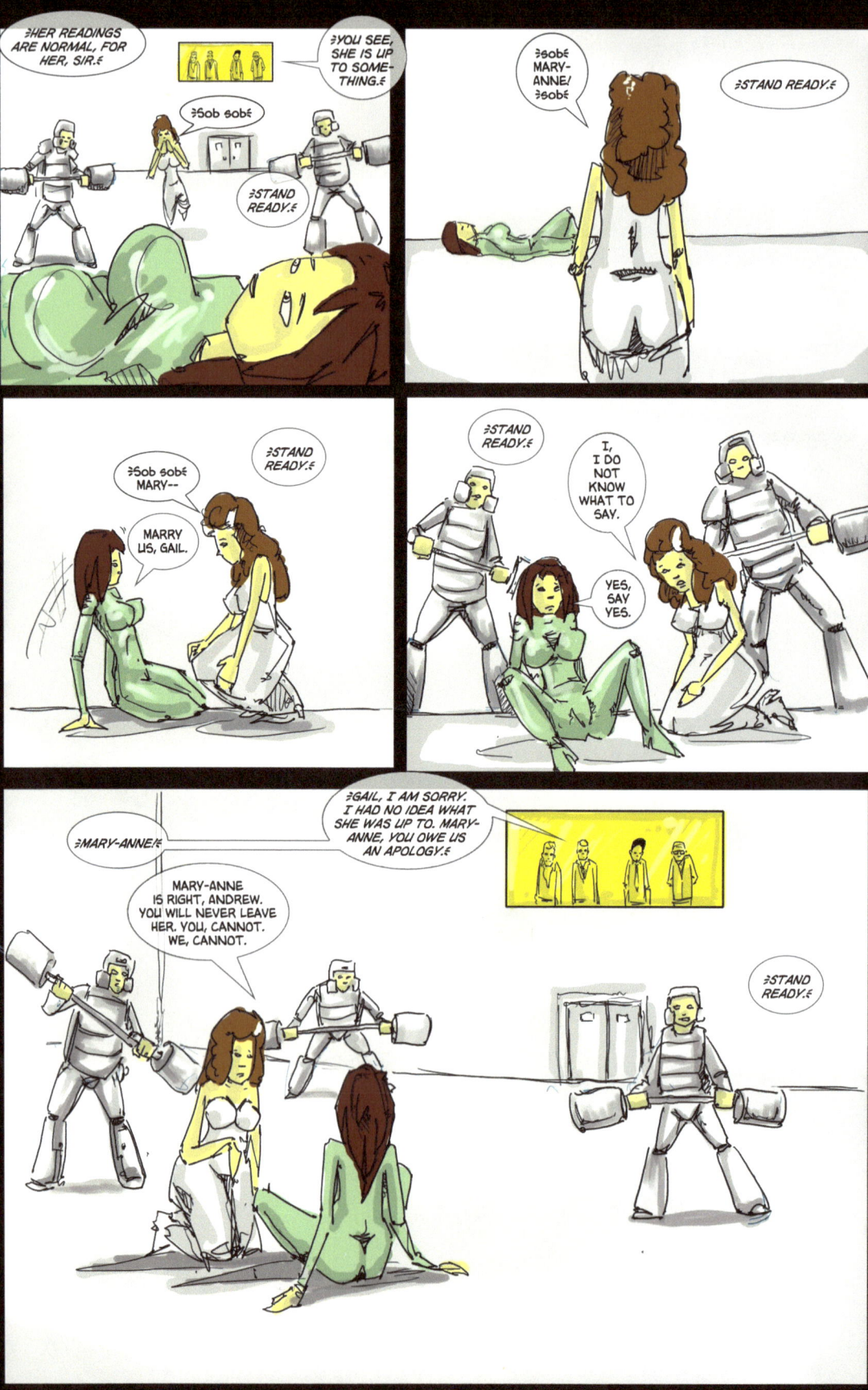

PO LYN LEE
OPHELIA HOUSE
NEXT ISSUE

"ASSASSINS"

FROM BIRD'S-EYE'S POINT OF VIEW,
WILLIAM CURTIS AND MI QUO REFLECT ON
THE PRESIDENCY, CRIMSON LOTUS, AND
MOTHER PI LYN. THE "TA SHEN LING" IS SEEN;
CAUGHT IN THE ACT, WHEN ANOTHER LITTLE
GIRL BEARS WITNESS TO THE "MI CHU"
PERFORMING ITS JOB. PO LEARNS THERE
IS MORE TO TOUCHING, THAN WHAT IS HELD
IN THE CARDS FOR ASSASSINS.

CARLTON L. SAMPSON

POET, GRAPHIC NOVELL AUTHOR.
CARLTON@POLYNLEE.COM
OTHER WORK AVAILABLE AT:
WWW.PHASCISTCLOWNS.COM

ANDREW L. WILLIS

AKA, THIOBIS THE ARTIST
FINE ART, SCULPTURE, ANIMATION,
MUSIC, AND WRITTEN.
ANDREW@POLYNLEE.COM
OTHER WORK AVAILABLE AT:
WWW.WAOOBAKEARTWORK.COM

COPY EDITOR "ROCKETMAN"

THE LINCOLN MEMORIAL
REFLECTING POOL

FROM BIRD'S-EYE'S POINT OF VIEW, WILLIAM CURTIS AND MI QUO
REFLECT ON THE PRESIDENCY, CRIMSON LOTUS, AND MOTHER PI LYN.
THE "TA SHEN LING" IS SEEN; CAUGHT IN THE ACT, WHEN ANOTHER
LITTLE GIRL BEARS WITNESS TO THE "MI CHU" PERFORMING ITS JOB.
PO LEARNS THERE IS MORE TO TOUCHING, THAN WHAT IS HELD
IN THE CARDS FOR ASSASSINS.

NEXT ISSUE

WWW.POLYNLEE.COM

www.ingramcontent.com/pod-product-compliance
Lightning Source LLC
Chambersburg PA
CBHW041001170626
46815CB00002B/110